BRAVE KIDS PRESS

THE EMOTIONS BOOK

A Little Story About **BIG** Feelings.

written by **Liz Fletcher**   illustrated by **Greg Bishop**

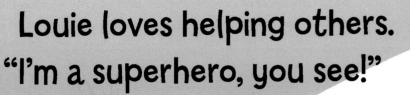

Louie loves helping others.
"I'm a superhero, you see!"

He brings smiles to everyone,
And kindness is the key.

But today something's different.
"I'm feeling a little strange."
Like when his sister hides his shoes

And his mommy makes him change.

"I have some new emotions,
And they have a lot to say.

Maybe I should listen
So I can get back to saving the day!"

"Hi there, I am anger.
I'm red, explosive, and mad!
And if you let me get too big
I can make you and others feel bad.

So when I come and visit you,
Let calmness be your friend.
Stop your body, breathe in deep,
You'll make good choices
in the end."

"And when I'm building up inside,
It might feel good to cry.
Perhaps you'll want a hug

Or just watch the clouds go by."

So when you feel me charging in,
Take one step at a time.
It's okay to take a break;
Things will turn out fine."

"I'm peaceful, bright, and green,
Like trees swaying in the breeze.

"And when you're calm and ready,
I will brighten up your day.

Hmmm, Louie thinks.
"My emotions are really great!

And when I understand them
They help me communicate."

So if you're ever feeling lost
Or not sure where to start,

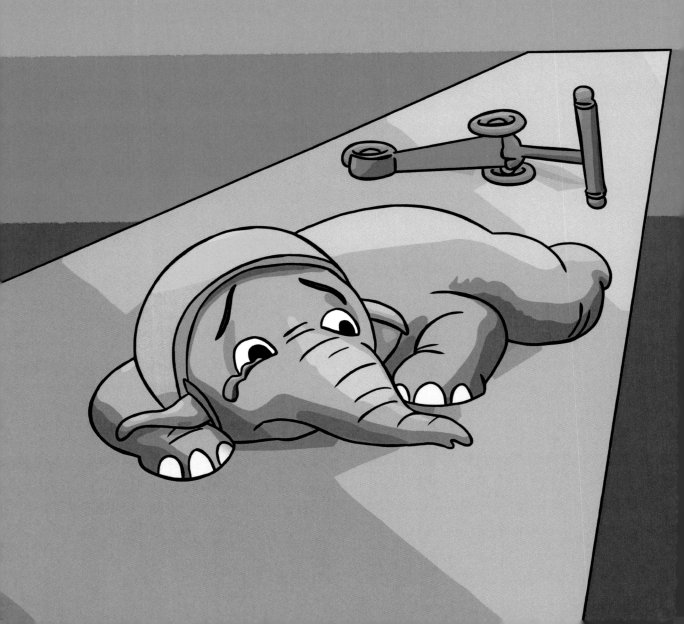

Just focus on your feelings,
And listen to your heart.

Now Louie knows his emotions!
He understands each one.
And when they work together,
There's much more time for fun!